MEG CABOT

Illustrated by Chesley McLaren

HARPERCOLLINS*PUBLISHERS*

Princess Lessons:

A Princess Diaries Book

Text copyright © 2003 by Meggin Cabot

Illustrations copyright © 2003 by HarperCollins Publishers Inc.
All rights reserved. No part of this book may be used or repro-
duced in any manner whatsoever without written permission except
in the case of brief quotations embodied in critical articles and
reviews. Manufactured in China. For information address
HarperCollins Children's Books, a division of HarperCollins
Publishers, 195 Broadway, New York, NY 10007.

www.harperteen.com

Library of Congress Cataloging-in-Publication Data
Cabot, Meg.

Princess lessons : a princess diaries book / Meg Cabot ;
illustrated by Chesley McLaren.

p.   cm. — (Princess diaries)

Summary: Princess Mia from "The Princess Diaries" offers
advice on inner and outer beauty, character development, etiquette, and dating.

ISBN 0-06-052677-7—ISBN 0-06-052678-5 (lib. bdg.)

1. Princesses—Juvenile literature. 2. Girls—Life skills guides—
Juvenile literature. 3. Girls—Conduct of life—Juvenile literature.
[1. Conduct of life.] I. McLaren, Chesley, ill. II. Title.
III. Series.

GT5390.C33 2003   2002012746
646.7—dc21   CIP
                                                           AC

Typography by Alison Donalty
17 SCP 20 19 18 17 16 15 14 13

❖

First Edition

Princess Lessons

A Princess Diaries Book

This book is for all the princesses-in-training out there.
Long may you reign.

A Royal Thank-You
to all who contributed to this book:
Jennifer Brown, Barb Cabot,
Alison Donalty, Barb Fitzsimmons,
Michele Jaffe, Josette "Twirly" Kurey,
Laura Langlie, Abby "Jou Jou" McAden, Chesley McLaren,
and especially royal consort Benjamin Egnatz
—M.C.

Many thanks to Alison Donalty, Barb Fitzsimmons,
Sasha Illingworth, Abby McAden, and Meg Cabot
for including me in such a royal project!
—C.M.

TABLE OF CONTENTS

INTRODUCTION

by Her Royal Highness Princess Mia Thermopolis

Ever since I found out that I am the heir to the throne of a small European principality (Genovia, population 50,000), there has been a *lot* of interest in what actually goes on during my princess lessons with my grandmother, the Dowager Princess Clarisse. I don't know why, because being a princess is actually very boring, and princess lessons with Grandmère pretty much—well—stink. I would much rather be a normal girl and be able to go to softball practice after school than have to go to princess lessons every day (not really, because I don't even like softball, what with my whole hand-eye coordination thing, but you get what I mean).

Anyway, seeing as how everybody keeps asking me, "Oh, Mia, can you please tell us the right way to curtsy?" and all, I figured I would share what I've learned during the long, grueling hours I've put in with Grandmère, so that you, too, can practice being a princess (though I honestly don't know why you would want to. See above re: stinkage factor).

Everything you need to know about posture and manners and how to address your subjects is here, if you're interested in that kind of thing. Did you know, for instance, that you never call a duke "My Lord"? No, it is always "Your Grace."

Since I am far from being an expert at this princess thing, I had to ask some of my friends and relatives to contribute stuff. And it turns out not even Grandmère knows everything about being a princess (only please don't tell her I said so).

The one thing I can't believe is that I am not even getting school credit for this. Which is so totally unfair, but whatever. Personal sacrifice is all part of the whole princess package, as you are about to find out.

Beauty

A Note from
Her Royal Highness Princess Mia

Real princesses always try to look their best—but, um, my best is probably totally different from yours. There are lots of different kinds of beauty. Like those models we see on magazine covers? A lot of people might hold them up as, like, the epitome of perfection and all of that, but just remember, in France it's considered beautiful *not* to shave under your arms.

So you see, beauty is really relative.

Princesses, like people, come in all different shapes and sizes. There is no one look that is right for everyone. Having a healthy body is way more important than having a body that looks good in low-rise jeans. And of course being a nice person is the most important thing of all. Throughout history, princesses have been remembered not for the waist size of their 501s, but for the good deeds they performed while they were on the throne.

There's one thing that looks good on everyone, though: confidence. Have confidence in yourself and your looks, and others will see your outer beauty as well as the inner.

That's what everybody keeps telling me, anyway.

PRETTY PRINCESS

by Paolo,
owner and proprietor of Chez Paolo, New York City

I, Paolo, am the one who turned the Principessa Amelia from Ugly Duckling into Swan. You, too, can look like a princess, if you follow Paolo's simple rules.

Beauty is *molto importante*, but so often overdone! A princess's look is *bella*, healthy, and well groomed. *Fresh* is the goal, and mascara, blush, and gloss are the tools that will get you there.

Everyone—especially I, Paolo—loves to play with makeup. But remember, a mask works only at Halloween!

Do not slather on foundation or eyeshadow unless you want to scare your populace (also, your parents won't like it so much, no?). Natural and bella is the way Paolo urges all you little principessas to go. If you want the dramatic look of black kohl and scarlet lipstick, join your school drama club (I spit on kohl). And do not come crying to Paolo if all the little princes, they run from you in horror. Only if you follow Paolo's way can you be assured *molto perfetto*!

PRINCESS ESSENTIALS

What every principessa should have in her handbag (besides cab fare, breath mints, emergency tiara, and hairbrush):

- Lipstick or gloss
- Pressed powder compact (to get rid of shiny nose)
- Concealer (for dark circles under eyes due to that late-night romantic tryst, no? Also for blemishes)
- Eye pencil

What every principessa should have in her bathroom (besides a phone and small television so she can keep abreast of world events even while bathing the royal body):

- Facial cleanser, exfoliator (or use a washcloth, but gently!), and moisturizer
- Astringent, toner, acne medication, beauty masks
- Foundation, concealer (for dark circles/blemishes)
- Eye shadow, liner (no kohl—Paolo spits on kohl!)
- Blush (natural color—unless you want to look like a clown principessa)
- Mascara
- Manicure set (nail polish, nail file, nail cutter)
- Hair products (shampoo, conditioner, styling products, etc.)

PAOLO'S PRINCESS BEAUTY REGIMEN

The look for royals? Fresh and clean! To get it, follow the beauty routine I designed for the Principessa Amelia:

1. Wash face morning and night with gentle cleanser. Follow with exfoliant, if needed (even royals get blackheads! No joke!), and blemish product or moisturizer.

2. Wash hair with gentle shampoo once a day, or every other day. Follow with conditioner. Use a wide-toothed comb to get out tangles. No one wants to see a bald principessa!

3. Hair products such as mousse or gel, used sparingly, can help control a mane gone wild or give body to thin hair. Find the product that works best for you by consulting a professional hair stylist, like me, Paolo, or by experimenting at home.

4. Bathe or shower daily. Principessas are known for smelling nice, no?

5. Deodorant/antiperspirant is a must! Whether you are playing croquet all day, or sitting under the hot lights of a television studio being interviewed by a famous news journalist, a principessa never lets them see her sweat—I mean, perspire.

6. Shave or wax unwanted body hair. The Principessa Amelia insists that this is a personal choice, and that women should not feel that they have to shave just to conform with "the societal mores of their culture." I, Paolo, could not disagree more strongly—even if you are French.

Waxing is messy and can cause rashes! It is best left to salon professionals like me, Paolo. Hair removal products like depilatories are expensive, smell bad, and don't remove all the hair. A good razor and lots of shaving cream is the way to go if you choose to be hair-free, as a principessa should be (even French ones).

And please, for Paolo, if you have hair growing from your upper lip or chin, pluck or bleach it (follow the instructions carefully on facial bleach packages). Never shave your face. No principessa should have razor burn over the lip!

7. Even nervous nail biters like the Principessa Amelia can have pretty nails! Keep them neatly trimmed and polished with clear gloss (dark polish makes nails look shorter). Pushing back the cuticles also can make bitten nails look longer.

Everyone is coming to Paolo, crying like a baby: "Oh, my hair is curly! Make it straight! Principessas have the straight hair!"

Well, I, Paolo, would like to say something:

Principessas can have curly hair. Principessas can have straight hair. Principessas can have dark hair. Principessas can have blond hair. Principessas may have cornrows, extensions, crew cuts, and dreads. The key to having the hair of a true principessa is:

A principessa's hair must be clean
A principessa's hair must not be in her eyes
A principessa's hair must not take more than
     fifteen minutes to style

Why this last rule? Because unless you have me, Paolo, to style your hair for you every morning, principessas have better things to do than mess around with their hair. If your hair is straight and you spend half an hour every morning curling it, then you waste your time! Straight hair can be very pretty. Same with curly hair. If you spend hours with a blow dryer trying to brush your hair straight, you waste more time!

Is it possible to be a principessa with green hair? Yes, so long as it is clean green hair, it is not hanging in the principessa's eyes, and it doesn't take longer than fifteen minutes for the principessa to style it.

Whatever look you come up with, make sure it is neat,

bella, and low maintenance. The last thing a principessa should ever be thinking about is her hair! Leave the worrying to me, Paolo! Because I, Paolo, am an artist. And my canvas is hair.

PAOLO

PRINCESS EYEBROWS

The eyes, they are the windows to the soul. If that is true, then the eyebrow is the curtain to the window of the soul. And who wants ugly curtains that look like you bought them at J.C. of Penney? Do you? No! That is why eyebrow maintenance is *molto importante*! We at Chez Paolo recommend plucking. Here is a quick guide to proper eyebrow-plucking technique:

Purchase a pair of tweezers, available in any drugstore, no?

Stand a little back from mirror, so you can see your whole face in a well-lighted room.

This is one case where less is NOT more. Do not overpluck! Remove only those hairs that extend past the inner corner of your eye, or which lie below the natural curve of the brow!

Tweeze unwanted hairs by pulling toward the ears (direction eyebrow hairs grow), so hair comes out more easily. What? You are crying? GOOD! The pain means it is working!

Brush brows upward and outward in the direction hairs grow. Fill in mistakes (and you will all make mistakes, as you are not Paolo) with eyebrow pencil in color that matches your hair.

Voilà! The perfect brow, courtesy of me, Paolo.

HER ROYAL HIGHNESS
PRINCESS MIA THERMOPOLIS ASKS:

CAN A PRINCESS WEAR BRACES?

Why not? Sometimes even princesses have imperfect teeth. While I myself do not have braces, I do have a retainer that I wear at night on account of the fact that I grind my teeth due to stress-related issues concerning my grades in a certain class. But that's another story.

Anyway, Paolo says the key to a beautiful smile while wearing braces is:

Brush often—nothing is more unregal than a bit of
    Gummy Bear wedged between the teeth
Use lots of gloss and pale lipstick (dark colors will
    draw attention to the mouth)
Play up the eyes (but not too much—mascara and a
    little glitter is really all you need)

Put it all together, and you've got: The perfect smile (with braces)!

II

Etiquette

Being a princess isn't just about how you look. A lot of it has to do with how you act. While knowing which fork to use may not *seem* very important, many an international incident has been prevented by good manners. At least according to Grandmère. Hopefully, by her spelling it all out here, you'll be able to avoid any social embarrassments or gaffes the next time YOU are dining with an ambassador or head of state.

MANNERS MATTER

by Clarisse Renaldo, Dowager Princess of Genovia

Having spent some time in America, I can only say that there appears to be an appalling lack of good manners in this country. Cab drivers honk without the least provocation, waiters can be so rude the fourth or fifth time you send back your Sidecar for refreshing . . . even so-called socialites exhibit a shocking unawareness of proper decorum, sometimes calling supper "dinner," and vice versa!

Etiquette is not, after all, only for royalty. It is for all of us! For only if we learn to treat one another with civility can we begin to hope for fuller global understanding and better treatment by wait staff.

PRINCESS POSTURE

Stand Like a Princess

If you wish to be treated like a princess, it is important that you look like one. Princesses never slouch. A princess stands tall at all times. Picture a string coming out from the top of your head and going to the ceiling. Imagine that someone is pulling that string, keeping your neck erect, your chin up. Shoulders should not be thrown back, however—you are a princess, not a fighter-jet pilot!

When being photographed from the feet up, assume the "model stance"— or third position in ballet (though without the extreme turnout). Your right foot should be forward, your left back and placed slightly behind the right. This will give your legs a slimmer appearance. Unless of course you are wearing slacks.

But really, a princess should never wear slacks to a photo shoot, unless she has thick ankles.

Sit Like a Princess

Princesses always keep their knees close together when sitting. This is so that the populace gathered before you in the throne room does not catch a glimpse of your unmentionables! Imagine that you are holding something very small between your knees—like a ten-carat sapphire ring from Tiffany, for instance. That is how closely they should be kept together. Your feet should be neatly crossed at the ankle, generally to one side, though directly beneath your chair is also correct.

In public, despite what my granddaughter might think, princesses never cross their legs; sit Indian style; rest their knees or feet on the chair in front of them; sit on one foot; sit with their knees spread apart (except when directed to do so in an emergency landing of the palace jet, of course); or sling their legs over an arm of their chair.

Hands should be folded demurely in the lap, unless you are doing needlepoint, signing documents of state, or unwrapping a well-deserved *cadeau* from an admirer.

Walk Like a Princess

A princess does not shuffle, skip, or saunter. She strides confidently, with her head held high, her gaze straight ahead, and her arms relaxed at her sides (except of course when she is holding a purse or small *chien*). Again, imagine that there is a string coming out from the center of your head, pulling you toward the sky. This is how a princess walks.

A princess's escort, be he consort or bodyguard, should always walk on the side of the princess that is closest to the street, to protect her from mud splashed by passing motorists, or a possible assassin's bullet.

ADDRESSING YOUR BETTERS

In Direct Conversation:

TITLE	CORRECT FORM OF ADDRESS
King or Queen	Your Majesty
Prince or Princess	Your Royal Highness
Niece, nephew, or cousin of the sovereign	Your Highness
Duke or Duchess	Your Grace
Earl, Marquis, Viscount, or Baron	My Lord
Countess, Marchioness, Viscountess, or Baroness	My Lady
Baronet or Knight	Sir (followed by first name)
Wife of Baronet or Knight	Lady (followed by first name)

COURTESY TITLES	CORRECT FORM OF ADDRESS
Son of duke, marquis, or earl	Lord (followed by first name)
Daughter of duke, marquis, or earl	Lady (followed by first name)
Children of lower peers, such as barons and knights	The Honorable (followed by first and last name, in indirect reference)

NONROYALS	CORRECT FORM OF ADDRESS
Boys under 18	Master
Men 18 and over	Mr.
Girls under 18	Miss
Women 18 and over	Ms.
Married women	Mrs. (unless they tell you otherwise)
Divorced women	Ms., or often Mrs. if using ex-husband's last name
Widows	Mrs.

[Except that you wouldn't call Jennifer Aniston "Mrs. Pitt," so I don't think this stuff works in real life. Maybe just call everyone "Ms."?]

[These comments you see in pink are from me, Princess Mia. Just so you know.]

INTRODUCTIONS TO ROYALS

It is all really very simple: When meeting royalty for the first time, commoners must bow or curtsy as they are introduced—particularly if they are residents of the country over which the person they are meeting is regent.

Everyone must bow or curtsy to a king or queen, but kings and queens do not have to bow or curtsy to people ranking below them, such as princes and princesses. Princes and princesses do not have to bow or curtsy to dukes and duchesses, dukes and duchesses do not have to bow or curtsy to earls and countesses, and so on. Americans do not have to bow or curtsy to anyone, because two hundred years or so ago they went to great trouble to disassociate themselves from the monarch who actually made their country possible . . . but Amelia asked me not to "get into that," so I will desist.

Still, it is polite to bow or curtsy to emperors, kings and queens, and princes and princesses, whether they rule over you or not.

The Perfect Curtsy

Place your left foot behind your right foot, and bend slightly at the knees, then stand up straight again. It is not necessary to fling one's upper torso onto the floor, as I understand some American debutantes like to do when they are introduced into society. A simple knee bend will do nicely, and you will have less of a chance of falling on your face.

The Perfect Bow

Keeping your shoulder and neck straight, bend forward at the waist, very briefly, then straighten up.

See? So simple.

[Principal Gupta, the head of Albert Einstein High, curtsied when she met Grandmère. It was the funniest thing I ever saw.]

INTRODUCTIONS TO NONROYALS

When you are introduced to someone for the first time, it is important to smile, look the person in the eye, and extend your right hand. Say, "Hello, I am Clarisse Renaldo, Dowager Princess of Genovia (or whatever *your* name happens to be)." When shaking hands, exert a confident, not overpowering grip. You are a princess, not a wrestler.

[But you don't want to have a wimpy grip either, or people will think you aren't self-actualized.]

When you are the one making introductions, be sure to include people's first and last names. If you can't remember someone's name, introduce the person whose name you do know ("Do you know His Royal Highness, Prince William?") and the person whose name you don't know will usually introduce themselves.

TALK LIKE A PRINCESS

Conversational DOs and DON'Ts

When meeting someone for the first time, begin by asking his/her advice or opinion. Do not ask him/her yes-or-no questions. Something like "In what region is your summer palace located?" or "What did you think of that scintillating article on the Japanese royal family in today's *New York Times*?" will do. Current events, popular movies, television shows, and music all make excellent conversation starters. You might also comment on the weather or the room in which you are standing.

[Only talk about the weather as a last resort. Weather is way boring.]

Do be a good listener:

Do not monopolize conversations, even if you *are* the only blue-blood in the room. Allow others to speak as well. Even if you are caught up in your own cleverness, remember to stop and ask your acquaintance about his opinion or experiences.

Do not gossip:

When you have just met a new person, it isn't smart to ask him something like "Did you hear about the countess and Prince René?" because he might reply, "No, the countess is my wife. What about her and Prince René?" Suddenly you will feel very uncomfortable.

Do not swear:
Princesses do not use curse words except under extreme provocation, such as the severing of a limb or the loss of a priceless piece of jewelry down the bidet.

[Princesses don't ridicule the looks, politics, religion, or extracurricular activities of others. Even cheerleading.]

EAT LIKE A PRINCESS

Formal Dining

It *will* happen. At some point you will be asked to a formal dinner. It is important that you familiarize yourself beforehand with the utensils that will be used.

Utensils are always positioned for use from the outside in (on the left of the plate) and the inside out (on the right of the plate). The first fork one reaches for is the one farthest from the plate. The opposite goes for knives on the other side of the plate. The knife closest to the plate is the knife used first, and so on.

[This is unlike the FOIL system in Algebra—First, Outside, Inside, Last. Always use the fork or knife closest to your left.]

Formal Place Setting (expected at state dinners, prom, etc.)

Service plate, positioned so pattern on plate
   faces diner
Butter plate, positioned above the forks at left
   of place setting
Wineglasses and water glass, above knives and
   spoons, on the right positioned by size
Salad fork, placed left of dinner fork
Meat fork, left of salad fork
Fish fork, left of meat fork
Salad knife, to the right of plate
Meat knife, right of salad knife
Fish knife, right of meat knife
Butter knife, positioned diagonally at top of
   butter plate
Soup spoon and/or fruit spoon, placed outside the
   knives
Oyster fork, beyond the spoons
Napkin

Understood? *Très bien!*

At a crowded dining table, the issue of which water glass, wineglass, or bread plate belongs to which diner can sometimes become confusing. This can be cleared up simply by forming your left thumb and index finger into the letter b and your right thumb and index finger into the letter d, as shown below.

b = bread   d = drink

The bread plate to your left is yours. The drinking glass to the right is also yours.

Voilà!

[You don't want to eat someone else's bread by mistake. You *really* don't want to drink from someone else's glass. Especially Boris Pelkowski's, which always has food floating in it.]

Dining DOs:

↪ Always wait until everyone is present at the table before taking your seat.

↪ Always place your napkin in your lap.

↪ Always wait until your hostess has lifted her fork before beginning to eat.

↪ Always cut food into bite-size pieces, using either the European style or the American style. In the European style, one cuts food by holding the knife in the right hand while securing the food with the fork in the left hand. Simply pick up the cut pieces of food with the fork still in the left hand, tines facing down. The American style is the same except that after cutting the food, lay the knife across the top edge of the plate and change the fork from the left to the right hand to eat, tines facing up. Either style is perfectly acceptable.

➛ Eat everything that is on your spoon or fork in one bite (take small portions).

➛ Remove seeds, bones, or pits from your mouth with your fingers (discreetly), and lay them on the side of your plate.

➛ Use your fingers to eat foods such as French fries, potato chips, sandwiches, and corn on the cob. Just be sure to wipe your fingers on a napkin after each bite—do not lick them.

➛ Always excuse yourself if you feel the need to leave the table midmeal. Place your napkin on your chair.

➛ When you are finished, lay your knife and fork beside one another across your plate, then wait for your hostess to rise before leaving the table yourself.

Dining DON'Ts:

⌐ Do not start eating until your hostess does.

⌐ Do not speak when your mouth is filled with food.

⌐ Do not lift your pinky when raising your glass.

[Even though Mrs. Thurston Howell III does this.]

⌐ Do not cut your meat (or any food) into bite-size portions before you begin eating. Cut off only what you intend to put into your mouth at that time.

⌐ Do not take huge mouthfuls of anything, no matter how good.

[Especially cold things, like sorbet.]

← Do not suck up the ends of noodles. Long pasta should be twirled into small bite-size portions on the end of the fork, against the bowl of a spoon or the edge of your plate.
← Do not re-dip a chip or crudité into a common bowl of dip if you have already taken a bite.

If, at a formal dinner—or even a casual meal with friends—you are offered a dish that you cannot or will not eat, simply say, "No, thank you," quietly and politely. No need to explain why, but if it is because of your staunch adherence to a vegan lifestyle, you may tell your hostess so, if you can do it without the whole table overhearing you. Otherwise, just say no, *merci*!

[It's not a good idea to try dropping something you are ethically opposed to eating, such as prosciutto-wrapped melon, onto the floor beneath your chair in the hope that your hostess's dog will scarf it up. Chances are the dog won't eat it either, and then it will just end up on the bottom of your shoe. Not that this ever happened to me.]

PRINCESS AND THE PEA (SOUP)

The dish that seems to confound most diners is not, as one might expect, the majestic lobster or prickly artichoke, but perhaps the simplest of all repasts: soup. Yes, soup. Between slurping and spoon-scraping, any number of disasters can ensue when soup is consumed incorrectly. The secret of soup is simple: away! Always spoon soup *away* from your person! Then lift the spoon to your mouth as you lean from the waist over the bowl. No hunching over the bowl like a doggie waiting for his kibble!

When the soup reaches your lips, sip it QUIETLY from the SIDE of the spoon. Contrary to popular opinion, in no culture is slurping EVER welcome. Not by royalty, anyway. And don't shove the whole spoon into your mouth as if you are swallowing down cough syrup. SIP from the side. SIP!

When the soup in your bowl is at a level that you must tilt the bowl to reach it, tilt the bowl AWAY from you. Get it? Spoon AWAY, tilt AWAY. That way you will avoid causing a spill of

Niagara Falls proportions into your lap.

And no blowing on your soup! If it is too hot to eat, WAIT FOR IT TO COOL. AND NO, YOU MAY NOT SPOON ICE FROM YOUR WATER GLASS INTO YOUR SOUP. In some countries, the chef would rightly consider this the gravest of insults, and be justified in throwing you out of his dining room.

TABLE TALK FOR A PRINCESS

Appropriate Table Conversation for a Princess

It is considered rude in most countries to talk about politics or religion at the dinner table, unless you are dining with close friends. People do not wish to have their appetites spoiled by listening to views that might differ radically from their own, no matter how much you may wish to enlighten them about the errors of their ways. Save such lecturing for the cocktail hour, during which your victims might reasonably fortify themselves against such an onslaught.

PARTY PRINCESS

Princesses are often called upon to entertain. Whether you are hosting a ball or a small, informal tea, the duties of a hostess are always the same:

→ Attempt to introduce guests who do not know one another, and engage them in a conversation that can be continued after you politely slip away to see to your other guests.*

*It is never a good idea to introduce guests with radically different political views to one another. A communist, for instance, should never be seated beside an anarchist during dinner. Unpleasantness is guaranteed to ensue.
[The same goes for cheerleaders versus nerds.]

➥ See that your guests are comfortable (it is inexcusable to leave off the air-conditioning on a hot day, or the heat on a cold one!) and provide ready access to food and drink.

➥ Mingle, mingle, mingle!

If you are the guest at a party:

➥ Arrive on time, or no later than fifteen minutes after the arrival time listed on the invitation. There is no such thing as "stylishly late"—just boorish!

➥ Members of the aristocracy are generally quite popular, and so are often invited to many events in a single night. In order to keep from showing favoritism to any one hostess, plan on spending about an hour at each ball or soiree—enough time for a cocktail. Dinner parties, however, are more difficult. Princesses should remain at a dinner party for at least one hour after a meal is served. Any departure earlier than this is vulgarly referred to by Americans as "dining and dashing." If not expected at any other events that night, you may safely remain at any party until everyone else is departing, or until your hosts begin to look noticeably fatigued. Then it is polite to take your leave. Be sure to find your host or hostess before you go, to thank them for inviting you. If he or she asks you not to leave, or encourages you to stay, you may do so if you are so inclined and you feel the invitation is sincere.

↬ If you wish to bring a friend or small *chien* who was not on the original invitation list, you must ask your host or hostess ahead of time if this is all right.

[This is especially important if some of the other guests (such as Boris Pelkowski) have allergies and might start sneezing uncontrollably at the introduction of animal dander into the immediate environment.]

Dear Grandmère,
The very generous check you sent me for
Christmas is going straight to the Save the
Whales fund! Thank you so much for helping me
to save an orca.

A written thank-you note is obligatory:

⟜ When you are the guest of honor at a dinner party or tribal ceremony

⟜ When you receive birthday, graduation, holiday, or coronation gifts

⟜ When you have stayed overnight with anyone who is not a close relative or friend whom you see frequently. A thank-you note is necessary in this case, even if you have thanked your host in person.

[For instance, I don't have to send a thank-you note to Shameeka for inviting me to her slumber party, but I do have to send one to Tante Simone for letting me spend the night in her villa.]

↜ When someone sends you flowers, particularly Get Well flowers

↜ When you receive notes of condolence from anyone

↜ When you receive a congratulatory note from anyone (for instance, upon your ascension of the throne)

The Sympathy Note

Princesses are often called upon to show strength in the most tragic of situations. When a member of Parliament or state dies, a princess's presence is required at the funeral. While it is no longer considered absolutely necessary to wear black at funerals, one should opt for muted colors, such as grays, browns, or beiges.

Additionally, princesses always send a written note of sympathy to the bereaved. Sympathy notes are much appreciated by people who have lost someone they love. Always handwritten, these notes should, if possible, contain an anecdote about the deceased that the reader can cherish:

> *Dear Tante Simone,*
> *I was deeply saddened to hear of the sudden death*
> *of your beloved cat, Monsieur Pomplemousse.*
> *Even though I didn't see Monsieur*
> *Pomplemousse all that often, I will never forget*
> *the time that I accidentally-on-purpose dropped*
> *my foie gras beneath my chair and he ate it all*
> *up so that I didn't have to. Monsieur*

*Pomplemousse really was a cat among cats, and
I know I will miss him terribly. Let me know if
there is anything I can do for you.*

   Love,
   Mia

Conversely, if someone close to you dies and you are the recipient of sympathy notes, you must acknowledge them in writing. The notes do not have to be long, but they must be sincere. A good example would be as follows:

*Cher Amelia,
Your kind note about Monsieur Pomplemousse
arrived at a time when I needed the support of my
family and friends. It is a great comfort to know
that Monsieur Pomplemousse was so beloved, and
I want to thank you for writing.*

   Sincerely,
   Her Highness Simone Grimaldi

PRINCESS ON THE PHONE

Even though the person on the other end of the telephone cannot see you, he or she can certainly hear you. It is important to practice proper telephone etiquette at all times.

If you are the one being called:

The best way to answer a telephone is by saying, "Hello." It is correct to ask, "May I ask who is calling?" if the person on the other end of the phone does not identify him- or herself right away. Furthermore, if the caller is not someone whose name or voice you recognize, you may inform him or her that the person they are trying to reach is busy and cannot come to the phone.

[Never admit to an unknown caller that you are alone in the house, particularly if your bodyguard has the day off!]

Call Waiting is convenient and in some homes, necessary. However, it is rude to keep anyone on hold for a long period of time. When answering Call Waiting, it is proper to say to the second caller, "I am afraid I have someone on the other line. May I call you right back?" Then remember to do so.

If you are the caller:

It is considered courteous and helpful to identify oneself immediately upon being greeted. The proper way to do this is by saying, "Hello, this is the dowager princess of Genovia. May I please speak to Prince René?"

Remember: Manners Matter!

PRINCESS PROTECTION

by Lars, Protection Specialist

There are some occasions when politeness doesn't count, and that's when you are in personal jeopardy. Princesses have bodyguards to protect them. But you don't necessarily need a six-foot-six-inch, two-hundred-and-eighty-pound (all hard muscle) Swedish expert in *krav maga* like me. You can protect yourself. It's easy!

When accosted by an adversary, remember to SING, by applying elbows or knees as hard as you can to your opponent's

> Solar plexus
> Instep
> Nose
> Groin

See? SING!!! It's easy! Anyone can do it.

Another excellent deterrent to physical attack is the use of the vocal cords. If someone whose motives appear suspicious approaches you, scream. Even if your adversary tells you to stop screaming, keep on screaming until help arrives. In general, screaming so confuses evil-doers, they flee the scene—like frightened little children.

III

Fashion

Sad but true: How you dress matters. It shouldn't—we should all be judged by how we behave, not by how we look. Still, people will totally judge you by what you wear. So you want to show your special uniqueness and own individual brand of style.

If you go to a school where you have to wear a uniform, like me, your day-to-day wardrobe is not really that big of an issue. If, however, you don't have uniforms where you go to school, then you have to put together what is called a "school wardrobe." School clothes are different from what you'd wear to, say, a ball or state dinner. Princesses' wardrobes differ drastically from normal people's, because princesses have to be on TV and get photographed a lot. I mean, you don't want to be wearing your favorite sloppy old sweatshirt while you're opening the children's wing you've donated to the local hospital. The doctors and patients will think you didn't care enough about the occasion to dress up . . . and that could cause an international incident (believe me)!

People who don't have to dress up every time they go out (like I do) are lucky. Still, even if you are just going to school, you should try to look cool, while still being comfortable.

LOOKING GOOD, FEELING BET*

by Sebastiano, celebrated Genovian fashion designer

So you want to look like a mod* for the first day of school? Good for you!

Remem* though . . . mods get paid to look good! Plus, they get a lot of their clothes for free, no? If you want to look like a mod on the bud* of a norm* girl, here is what you can do:

Shop at the outs.* Everyone has outs somewhere near their home. Very good deals can be found at outs.

*Because English is not Sebastiano's first language, he has some difficulty pronouncing the second syllables of many English words. In this case, Bet means Better. Also: *model *remember *budget *normal *outlets

58

Save your mon* all sum* and then one day before school starts, go with friends to an out. When you get to the out, don't just spend, spend, spend. Buy what you need.

What ev* girl needs for back-to-school ward* is this:

- One pair good-fit jeans, blue
- One pair good-fit jeans, black
- One pair good-fit slacks, any color
- Two sweat* sets, any color
- Two blouse, any color
- T-shirts, many colors
- 1 skirt, above the knee (but not too much)
- 1 skirt, below the knee (but above ankle)
- Socks, any colors
- Tights/panty*
- Bras, under*
- One pair slip-on shoes, low heel
- One pair ten* shoes
- One pair slip-on shoes, higher heel
- One pair boots, knee-high
- One ski jack*
- One black coat, knee-length

*money *summer *every *wardrobe *sweater *pantyhose
*underwear *tennis *jacket

You should be able, from the previous list, to put togeth* a doz* or so great looks that will last all year. Mix and match! Use your imag*! Be creat*! Bor* your moth's* scarves and necks*! Wear them wrap* around your head! Who cares what peop* say? If they no like your outfits, they no like Sebastiano, no? Experi* with fash* is only way to know what look is best for you. Only please, for Sebastiano's sake, no princess would ever wear:

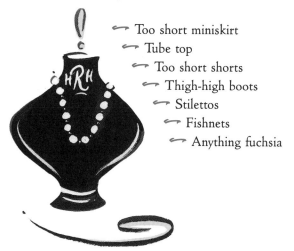

← Too short miniskirt
← Tube top
← Too short shorts
← Thigh-high boots
← Stilettos
← Fishnets
← Anything fuchsia

[Sebastiano has obviously never been to a dance at Albert Einstein High School.]

*together *dozen *imagination *creative *borrow
*mother's *necklaces *wrapped *people *experimenting
*fashion

DRESS LIKE A PRINCESS

by Her Royal Highness Clarisse Renaldo,
Dowager Princess of Genovia

How you look on the outside reflects how you feel on the inside, and a slovenly appearance symbolizes an uncultured mind. All the truly great thinkers of the past century—Princess Grace of Monaco, Audrey Hepburn, and of course, Eva Gabor—were always impeccably dressed. So put away your dungarees and tennis shoes and prepare to learn how to dress like a royal.

[Plato was a great thinker, and all he ever wore was a bedspread.]

Lingerie

Bras in tones of white or neutral—as well as one in black, but only to be worn with that essential little black dress. Never, never, never wear a black bra with a white shirt.

[This assumes, of course, that you actually have something to put in a bra, unlike me.]

Girdles, again in white or neutral. One black, for above-mentioned dress.

[Girdles! I suppose she means control-top panties. Why a princess should be forced to conform to the Western standard of idealized beauty—the androgynous silhouette—is beyond me; although the Duchess of York tried that whole letting-it-all-hang-out thing, and it didn't really work out for her.]

Slips: one black (again for aforementioned dress), one of white cotton to be worn starched under full summer skirts.

[Slips are what they had before anyone invented Static Guard. Although it is probably better just to wear a slip than to use Static Guard, due to the release of fluorocarbons contributing to our rapidly disintegrating ozone layer.]

Basics

Five or more suits in muted tones of blue or gray, for luncheons, teas, meetings of state, secret assignations, etc.

[Suits are to Grandmère what T-shirts and jeans are to the rest of us.]

Black dress of taffeta, silk, light wool, velveteen, or faille.

[Except that Grandmère says it is inappropriate for girls under the age of eighteen to wear black unless they are attending a state funeral. Um, *hello*. Clearly, Grandmère has never been below Fourteenth Street, where, if you are not wearing black and do not have at least one tattoo, you stick out like a PETA member at a bullfight.]

Formal gown, in tones of pale blue, pink, white, or jonquil.

[No red. Never red, unless you want to look like Nancy Reagan.]

Camel-hair coat: The perfect coverall from morning to night. Look for a box cut or flare cut to slip easily over skirts with crinolines.

[Contrary to what I first thought, camel-hair coats aren't actually made from real camel hide, so you don't have to worry about having murdered a dromedary while wearing one. Oh, I almost forgot: CRINOLINES!!! HA HA HA HA!!!]

Chinchilla cape: No princess should be without one.

[Um, excuse me, but have you ever seen a chinchilla in a pet store? They are the cutest, cuddliest animals you can imagine. Like chipmunks that got rolled in cotton candy. Wearing a cape made out of hundreds of little dead chinchillas? Yeah, so not something this princess would ever do.]

Raincoat: Because sometimes, in spite of everything, it rains, even on princesses.

Shoes

Loafers, preferably hand sewn, and from Italy.

[I think it is okay to wear shoes made out of leather because people—not me, but other people—eat beef, so at least you know the cows aren't being slaughtered merely for their hides.]

One pair of black pumps, heel no higher than two inches.

[Especially if a two-inch heel will make you as tall as your boyfriend. Not that there's anything wrong with that.]

Evening sandals of gold or silver to be worn with formal gown.

[The preferred shoe for *this* princess is black leather, with yellow stitching. Yes, I am talking about combat boots! Combat boots are the most comfortable thing you can wear (that's why soldiers wear them: they have to march for miles and miles, sometimes in inclement weather).

Plus combat boots make a statement. They say: I refuse to conform to the petty rules laid out by society's fashionistas. I am just me, Mia Thermopolis, princess, Greenpeace-supporter and high school student!!!!]

Combat boots are not suitable footwear for a princess.

Accessories

Simple strand of perfectly matched pearls for everyday wear.

[Did you know that when a pearl is extracted from an oyster, the oyster dies? So really, if you wear pearls, there is a pile of dead oysters somewhere.]

Matching pearl stud earrings.

[Two dead oysters.]

Tasteful diamond studs, no smaller than one carat each, no larger than three—a princess is never flashy.

[I learned in World Civ that it is really important to make sure that your diamonds were not mined in a foreign country that uses child slave labor or engages in guerrilla warfare with neighboring villages. This is something I have noticed they do not mention in those Diamonds Are Forever ads.]

Tiara, seventy-five carats at least, for formal occasions.

[See child labor/guerrilla warfare comment re: diamond studs.]

White cotton elbow-length gloves.

[These are actually very handy. When you are wearing white gloves no one can see how badly you bit your fingernails while you were watching *Smallville*.]

With a wardrobe of these items, no woman—peasant or princess—can ever go wrong. From royal weddings to Wimbledon, she will always be dressed to perfection. And looking the part is, of course, key to *being* the part.

[But I think it might be more princesslike if you took the money you would have spent on this wardrobe and donated it to Bide-A-Wee, the animal welfare organization whose no-kill adoption centers have found homes for more than one million unwanted pets in the century they have been in operation. But that is just my opinion.]

Grandmère's ideal

Mia's reality

PROPER TIARA MAINTENANCE

An essential part of any young princess's wardrobe is, of course, her tiara. There are many different types of sparkling head ornaments, from the decorative comb to the ermine-lined papal miter. But perhaps the most recognizable archetype of princesshood is the tiara.

Tiaras are correctly worn approximately two to three inches from the beginning of the hairline. Too close to the hairline gives one a slightly Neanderthalic look: too far back, and the tiara will not be visible in those all-important photos released to the press.

A tiara may never be worn at breakfast. In fact, it is gauche to don one's tiara before eleven in the morning, except in the event of a state funeral or royal wedding.

Additionally, tiaras must not be worn:

- Swimming
- Horseback riding
- Waterskiing
- Beneath hard hats while touring construction sites
- During a coup d'état

[Also, it's a good idea not to take your tiara out of its carrying case while you're in a moving vehicle or on a plane, because it could fly out of your hand and poke an innocent bystander in the eye. Not that this ever happened to me. Except that one time.]

IV.

Contentment Happiness Acceptance Joy CREATIVITY PEACE Motivation Purposefulness Health

Character

You are probably as surprised as I was to find out that being a princess isn't all about being graceful and having good manners and what you wear. There's a bunch of other stuff, involved, too . . . like being kind to those who are less fortunate than you, and being socially aware. This type of thing is called Character.

You don't have to have been born royal to have good character. In fact, I know a bunch of people who aren't in the least bit royal who have a lot of very princesslike qualities.

They, like me, are striving to achieve self-actualization. How do you achieve self-actualization? Well, here are some tips that might help you along your way.

JUNGIAN TREE OF
SELF-ACTUALIZATION

To gather the FRUITS of life, you must start by growing a solid foundation of ROOTS:

Acceptance   Peace   Creativity
Contentment   Purposefulness Fulfillment
Health   Self-motivation Happiness
Joy

Jungian theory states that by developing the characteristics below, you will reap the awards above:

Compassion   Love   Enthusiasm
Charity   Warmth   Forgiveness
Friendship   Kindness   Gratitude
               Trust

See? It's easy. Be a nice person, and you will not only seem like a princess, but you'll also achieve complete spiritual harmony!

HOW TO MAKE A FRIEND

*by Hank Thermopolis, male supermodel and recent
transplant to New York City from Versailles, Indiana*

So you are starting at a new school/modeling agency and
you don't know anyone. That ain't an excuse to just go sit
in a corner by yourself! The only way you're gonna make
friends is to be . . . well, friendly! Smile at people. Say
howdy. Don't butt in on anybody's private conversation, but
if you overhear a group of folks talkin' about a movie you
just saw, say, "Hey! I saw that! Wasn't it cool when that
giant alien bit off that guy's head?" or something like that.

If you're one of them shy types, try this: Find another
shy type. When she's off by herself with her head stuck in
a library book, go up to her and be all, "Howdy, I'm new
here. Can you tell me where the portfolio drop-off is?"
Sure, she might tell you to get lost. But chances are she
won't. Then you've just made a friend!

Remember, making friends is only part of it. You have
to keep 'em, too. How do you do this, you ask? Well, by
being loyal, never betraying 'em, and not forgettin' 'em,
even after there's a giant billboard of you half-nekked in
Times Square.

BE A SPORT

by His Royal Highness
Prince René Phillipe August Giovanni

There's more to good sportsmanship than just being a good athlete. You also have to set a good example for others (if you've had the good fortune to be born a royal prince like me, anyway). This means not being a sore loser. Royals never throw temper tantrums on the playing field, accuse others of cheating, or throw their polo mallets when they lose. They accept defeat graciously, giving the winner a handshake and a sincere, "Good game." Princes don't complain about the condition of the playing field or a decision from the ref, however warranted such complaints might be.

When a prince wins a game, he never gloats, does a special dance when he scores a goal, or sings rude songs about the losers. A good winner always acknowledges his opponent's effort, and remembers that he himself could easily be in the loser's place.

Whether skiing, sailing in a regatta, or merely playing a game of billiards in the palace game room, a prince always plays his best, is enthusiastic, and tries to have a good time—no matter how badly he might be losing.

HOW TO BE A GOOD SPECTATOR

by Lilly Moscovitz, avid moviegoer and
girlfriend of a mouth breather

Let's face it: there is **NOTHING** more annoying than paying your ten dollars (more if you live in Canada or have purchased popcorn and soda) and sitting down in a movie theater, only to have the people behind you talk loudly or kick your chair all through the feature. This is **NOT** princess behavior. It is not even human behavior.

When people gather together in a public place to enjoy a sporting event, movie, play, or concert, they have usually paid the price of a ticket for their entertainment. So it's totally uncool for other people to try to ruin these gatherings by chewing loudly, yelling stuff at the movie screen (well, okay, this can be fun at a premiere or Rocky Horror, or whatever, but not ALL the time), answering cell phone calls, talking to each other, screaming obscenities at players on the opposing team, or SMOKING.

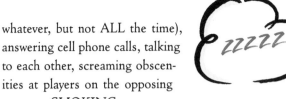

A word to mouth breathers: So you have a deviated septum or have to wear a bionater. Still, do you HAVE to breathe out of your mouth? DO YOU??? Could you TRY putting your lips together and breathing out of your nose??? PLEASE???

We all have to live on this planet. Let's try to not get on each other's nerves.

YOU'VE GOT MAIL

by Kenneth Showalter, e-mail afficionado

Everybody loves e-mail. I don't know anyone who goes, "Oh, no, not again," when he sees messages in his IN box. People like getting e-mails, so long as they aren't flames or spam.

I guess the best thing about e-mail, besides the fact that it is a speedy, fun way to communicate with your friends, is that it is an excellent method—if you don't feel comfortable talking face-to-face with members of the opposite sex—to communicate with the person you secretly admire. Of course, certain precautions need to be observed if you don't want to come on too strong:

← Stop e-mailing someone who doesn't e-mail back. That means he or she isn't interested.

← Excessively long e-mails or too many e-mails in a twenty-four-hour period can be a turnoff for someone who doesn't feel the same way about you that you feel about them.

← Don't e-mail back the minute you receive a response. You don't want your crush to think you have nothing better to do than sit around checking your e-mail every five minutes (even if that's true). Also, part of the fun of e-mail is wondering if/when you're going to get a reply. Make her wait a little!

Remember, e-mail is a great way to communicate . . . but there's a difference between getting to know someone and, well, stalking them. TTYL!

[If the person you admire is someone you have met in a chat room, keep in mind that they could actually be a mouth-breathing psycho or a double agent from a rival kingdom, or something. Proceed with grave caution.]

POPULARITY

by Shameeka Taylor, friend of Princess Mia Thermopolis and recently appointed AEHS cheerleader

Everyone wants to be popular. But as hard as some of us work at it, it just isn't happening. I mean, Mia Thermopolis is a princess, and she isn't popular. I tried out for the cheerleading squad, and even though I made it and everything, I'm still not popular. Not that I want to be. That's not why I tried out for the squad. I just wanted to see if I could do it. And I did.

I don't think anyone understands why it is, exactly, that some people are popular and some aren't. I mean sometimes totally plain girls are voted Homecoming Queen, while really beautiful girls aren't even asked to the dance, so it isn't really about how you look. And total jerks have been elected president of their class, while nice guys sit home watching *Deep Space Nine* every Saturday night, so it isn't about how you act, either.

I guess being popular is more about an attitude. From what I've observed, the less people seem to care about being popular, the more popular they are. So worrying about where you stand in the social hierarchy of your school is pretty silly. It's more important to have *good* friends than popular ones, and to do your own thing without caring what anybody else thinks. That's the only way to achieve that self-actualization thing that Mia is always talking about—at least that I know of.

[Even though Shameeka joined the cheerleading squad, we forgive her because she has proved *some* cheerleaders *are* nice (also, now she can give us all the dirt on Lana!).]

FIVE EASY WAYS YOU
CAN SAVE THE PLANET

by Her Royal Highness Princess Mia Thermopolis

Princesses want to make sure this planet and all the species on it stick around for a while. By following the simple steps below, you can help, in a small way, to make sure it does:

1. Walk. Ride a bike. Or take public transportation, if they have it where you live. Save our vital natural resources.

2. You know those plastic things that come around cans of soda when you buy a six-pack? Clip the holes so they aren't holes anymore, then throw it away. Sometimes those things get into the ocean and dolphins' noses accidentally slip through those holes, and they get stuck with their mouths closed, and they can't eat anything and they starve to death.

3. Recycle. It isn't hard. The cans go in a bag. The newspapers get tied up.

4. Support candidates who want to protect the environment. Even if you are too young to vote, you can volunteer for candidates who are working to make the air safe for all of us to breathe.

5. DON'T LITTER!!!

MIA THERMOPOLIS AND LILLY MOSCOVITZ'S LIST OF MOVIES IN WHICH CHARACTERS ACHIEVE SELF-ACTUALIZATION AND/OR OTHERWISE BEHAVE IN A PRINCESSLIKE MANNER

Vision Quest: Matthew Modine stays true to himself, despite being dumped by Linda Fiorentino, and wins the wrestling tournament (as well as the heart of Daphne Zuniga), all while wearing a cute, form-fitting body stocking.

The Matrix: Keanu Reeves chooses saving mankind over lying around dreaming about steak.

Crazy/Beautiful: Kirsten Dunst has to come to terms with her relationship with her father, or he will send her to a camp for troubled teens and she will never see her hottie boyfriend again.

Legally Blonde: Reese Witherspoon slowly comes to the realization that knowledge is more important than bridal registries, while still managing to look fabulous the whole time.

Bring It On: Cheerleaders (headed by Kirsten Dunst) learn that winning isn't everything: sometimes doing the right thing is more important.

Save the Last Dance: A ballet dancer (Julia Stiles) finally admits that just because her mom died on the way to her Juilliard audition is no reason to hang up her toe shoes.

Spider-Man: Tobey Maguire proves that just because you have the ability to dominate the earth doesn't mean you should. A valuable lesson for all world leaders!

V

Education

*A Note from
Her Royal Highness Princess Mia*

Contrary to popular belief, you don't need to have gotten straight A's in high school to rule a country. You don't have to have gone to high school at all—especially if you inherit a throne, the way I'm going to someday.

Sadly, however, there will be those (like my dad, who says I still have to go to college, despite the fact I already have the princess career all lined up) who will insist upon your not only finishing high school, but on receiving a secondary education as well. And really, if you think about it, it's probably good to learn about world history and math, etc., so you'll at least have some idea what you're doing when you meet with Parliament and sign tax bills into laws and stuff.

So far, high school has been the worst experience of my life (not including the whole princess thing). Anybody who says these are the best years of your life is probably someone who was popular or something when they were in high school.

APPROPRIATE EDUCATION FOR A MONARCH-TO-BE

by Her Royal Highness Clarisse Renaldo,
Dowager Princess of Genovia

The prevailing assumption when I was a girl was that young ladies needed only to be sent to school to receive a formal education if they were homely or had no other way of meeting eligible young men.

Today things are so very different. I think it is vital that girls learn at school the important skills that are sometimes neglected by their mothers. Every princess-in-training needs a thorough education in the following:

↪ Latin (in order to read the family crests of her peers)

↪ French (so that she will understand the sweet nothings being whispered in her ear; also the menu at Lespinasse)

↪ Needlepoint (embroidery, *petit-point*, crochet—a lady's hands never rest)

↪ Dancing (waltz, rumba, tango)

↪ Gemology (so that she can tell a fake from the real thing)

Proper familiarity with the above will guarantee any girl a lifetime of thrilling romantic encounters and exotic adventures.

Every girl needs to learn to ballroom dance . . .

. . . so she won't look like a loser at the prom.

APPROPRIATE EDUCATION
FOR A MONARCH-TO-BE

by His Royal Highness Prince Artur Christoff Phillipe
Gerard Grimaldi Renaldo of Genovia

The responsibilities facing world leaders today are mind-boggling. Only through contributing to the global good by strengthening democratic governance shall we put an end to tyranny and dictatorship. Effective professionals in international service and governance today need a thorough understanding of theory and history as well as superior analytical and practical skills. Anyone hoping for a career in the public service, or even to help solve problems facing public servants today, must have at least a passing familiarity, if not an actual degree, in the following:

- Economic Policy
- Bioethics
- Quantitative Business Analysis
- Fiscal Decentralization and Local Government Finance
- Comparative Income Tax Design
- Analytic Frameworks for Policy
- Agribusiness and Food Policy
- Privatization, Finance, and the Regulation of Public Infrastructure
    - Negotiating EU Enlargement
    - Viable Communities and Public Safety
    - Environmental and Resource Science
    - Justice and Public Policy Issues
    - Designing and Managing Energy Systems
    - Education Policy and Urban School Reform
    - Human Rights, State Sovereignty, and Persecution
        - War and Ethnic Conflict
    - Law and Politics of International Conflict Management
        - Force and State Craft
            - Intervention and Peacekeeping
            - Gaining and Using Institutional Power
                - Leadership in the Face of Conflict

- Multi-Party Dispute Resolution
- Intelligence, Command, and Control
- Defense Resource Allocation and Force Planning
- Controlling Proliferation of Weapons of
Mass Destruction

Through careful diplomacy, the seeds of international peace have been sown. Only through education will peace flourish. The fate of the world is in YOUR hands. Do not fail us.

EXTRACURRICULAR ACTIVITIES

by Lana Weinberger, Captain,
Junior Varsity Cheerleading Squad and
Most Popular Girl at Albert Einstein High School

Extracurriculars aren't just something you do after school to meet boys (although that is an added plus). No, colleges look at your transcripts to see whether or not you were involved in after-school activities.

Some extracurricular activities that you might consider taking part in are cheerleading (if you are pretty and flexible enough), soccer, gymnastics, crew, lacrosse, track, basketball, football, baseball, or volleyball.

Some of the geek extracurriculars are yearbook, the school paper, drama club, choir, chess club, computer club, etc.

And if you are a true dork, you can volunteer after school for organizations like Meals on

Wheels, Greenpeace, your local library, hospital, or home-less shelter. Colleges really like that kind of thing, even though it mostly means you have to be around people you normally wouldn't be caught dead with.

And now I would just like to take this opportunity to ask all of you to please stop hogging the mirror every day in the girls' room, because it is really hard for me to get in there and check my lip gloss.

[What Lana doesn't seem to realize is that all the so-called geeks in our school today are tomorrow's Bill Gateses, George Clooneys, and Steven Spielbergs. By alienating them she is only making it that much more unlikely that any of them will look her way at our future class reunions.]

The MYSTERIOUS WORLD OF GUYS

*A Note from
Her Royal Highness Princess Mia*

So you've finally found your handsome prince . . . or at least a guy you'd like to get to know better. Here are some ways you can attract his attention without causing him to run from you and your ardor like a startled fawn, from romance expert (she has read more than one thousand romance novels!) and fellow high schooler Tina Hakim Baba.

Also included: a contribution from special guest Michael Moscovitz (that's right . . . MY ROYAL CONSORT).

I WANT *YOU* TO RIDE OFF INTO THE SUNSET WITH PRINCE CHARMING: HERE'S HOW YOU CAN MAKE IT HAPPEN!

by Tina Hakim Baba, high school romance specialist

Seven secrets to securing your true love's heart, or at least a date with him:

1. Look neat and pretty around the object of your affections. Clearly this is not possible if the two of you have the same gym class, but you know what I mean: Try to look as neat and pretty as possible, within reason.

2. Be friendly, but do not come on too strong: Smile at the guy, and say hi when you see him. If an opportunity for conversation crops up, seize it, but do not go out of your way to make this happen. (For instance, don't pretend to bump into him then drop your tiara. Most of the time, boys can see through ploys like this.)

3. Once you have made his acquaintance, try to keep things light. Don't blurt out all your problems—no matter how interesting or dramatic you might think they are—or gossip

in a mean way. Remember, you are trying to impress him with your wit and charm, not scare or repulse him.

4. Don't forget to listen when it's his turn to say something. There is nothing more irresistible than a good listener. A good listener:

- Never interrupts
- Makes eye contact
- Lets the person say everything he or she has to say before speaking herself

5. Don't get upset if you have a lot of conversations with the same guy and he still doesn't ask you out. Boys do not mature as rapidly as girls, and he may not even be thinking along those lines yet.

6. You may need to resort to more drastic measures, such as joining the same club he belongs to, or showing up at the same events he attends, before he finally notices you. There is nothing wrong with feigning an interest in, say, arachnids, if he is a spider lover. But it is usually better once you are going out to admit

that you don't really care for eight-legged creatures . . . just for him! He will probably be flattered. Just make sure you genuinely *do* have a few things in common, or you'll end up spending a lot more time than anyone would care to in the insect house at the zoo or watching tarantula documentaries on the Discovery Channel.

7. If, after all of this, the guy still hasn't asked you out, you may need to take the bull by the horns (so to speak), and ask him out yourself.

Tina on: Asking a Guy Out . . .

According to Mia's grandmother, it is never okay for a girl to ask a guy out. No offense to the dowager princess, but this isn't true. The only thing that is never okay is to keep asking out someone who consistently turns you down. He is turning you down for a reason, and that reason may be that he isn't interested in you in that way; he likes someone else; he's not allowed to date outside his own faith; or he's betrothed to another. Try not to take his refusal personally (even though I know it's hard not to) and move on. Who knows? Eventually he might come to his senses (but by that time you'll probably have found the love of your life!).

Six secrets that will help turn that *No, thanks* into an *I can't wait*:

1. Study dates are good because they are low pressure. For instance, you can ask a guy to come over (while your parents are home) so that the two of you can quiz each other for your World Civ exam. Group dates are also an excellent way to get to know someone. Going ice skating, out to eat, or to the movies in a large group is fun and less intimidating than one-on-one dating when you are just

beginning to get acquainted with someone.

2. Ask the guy out to a specific event scheduled for a specific date. Don't say, "Do you want to hang out sometime?" This is bad because there is no polite way he can get out of it if in fact he likes someone else. Instead, ask, "Would you like to attend my coronation with me on Saturday night?" This way, if he likes you, but he is busy Saturday night, he can say, "Sorry, I can't. But I can go Sunday." Or, if he doesn't like you, he can just say, "Sorry, I can't."

3. Generally you should ask someone out two to three days before the event—at least a week or more in advance if it is a special event, like the Prom. It is rude to call someone on Saturday night and ask them out for that evening, unless it is for a casual group thing. To wait until the last minute to ask someone out implies that you assumed he or she did not have other plans.

4. Ask him out in person, over the phone, or through e-mail. Don't have someone else ask him out for you because you're too chicken to ask him yourself! No one likes a scaredy-cat. Besides, if he says no, all these other people will know about it, and you will be mortified.

5. Ask when he is alone, not hanging out with a group of friends. Most guys are pretty immature, and give each other a hard time about these things. Spare him—and yourself—the agony. And if you are calling, call at a decent hour, like before nine in the evening. No need to get his parents upset before they've even met you!

6. Generally, the person who does the asking is the person who does the paying. Never ask a guy out and expect HIM to pay your way! If you are not prepared to pay his way, make sure he knows that in advance, so he brings enough money. For instance, you might say, "Want to go bowling at Chelsea Piers on Friday night? I'll pay for the pizza if you pay for the shoes and games."

Tina says: If HE Asks YOU Out . . .

You lucky girl! He asked! He finally asked! Now don't blow it by jumping around, pumping your fist in the air. Be enthusiastic, but be cool.

[If you are like me, and your father, the prince of a small European country won't allow you to go out with a boy he hasn't met, you must confess this IMMEDIATELY to any boy who asks you out. It is not fair to the boy just to spring it on him at the last minute. He needs time to prepare mentally, because meeting monarchs can be very intimidating.]

Tina's Five Possible Answers to the Big Question:

1. If you have to check with your parents before accepting a date, say, "Oh, I'd love to go to the planetarium with you on Saturday, but I have to check with my mom first. May I call you back when I know for sure?" Then be sure to call him back promptly.

2. Once you have said yes to a date, it would be very unprincesslike to change your mind and cancel at the last minute because:
a) someone you like better has asked you out, or
b) you decide you do not like the boy as much as you thought.
     You HAVE to go on the date. Canceling is only acceptable if you become ill or there is an unavoidable family emergency, like a coup in your kingdom. If either of these things happens, you must call your date at once to let him know. Never, ever just fail to show up on a date. Think how you would feel if someone did that to you!

3. If someone you don't particularly like asks you out, think before you say no. Sometimes people don't make very good first impressions, or act differently around other people than they do when they are just with one other person. That boy in your Lit class who cracks all the jokes may not be as cute as the slightly dim guy who sits next to you in World Civ, but remember it is more fun to laugh than it is to gaze at a chiseled profile.

4. If you really can't stand the guy who's just asked you out, say, "I'm so sorry, but I already have other plans." You don't need to elaborate, or invent complicated lies. For instance, if you say, "I'm sorry, I have to christen a battleship that night," and then the guy sees you at the movies instead, his feelings will be hurt. And princesses try never to hurt other people's feelings. That's why a princess would never call every single one of her friends after turning down a date and go, "You'll never believe who just asked me out." A princess tries to treat others the way she would like to be treated.

5. If someone you do like asks you out but you can't go because you already have something scheduled for that evening, you need to convey your regret sincerely, so he'll ask you out some other time. Say, "I am so sorry I can't, I have to assume my place on my rightful throne that night. But I'm free next weekend, if the invitation is still open." This way, he will know you really do want to go out with him, and are not just making up an excuse.

Everybody gets dumped. Even totally gorgeous movie stars like Nicole Kidman. Even princesses.

Here is what you should do while you are waiting for your heart to heal: Throw yourself into some fun extracurricular activities. Join your school drama club, or volunteer at your local no-kill animal shelter, or take up karate, or get a part-time baby-sitting job and watch dopey Disney movies with the kids. Do something— ANYTHING—to get your mind off the guy.

Which is not to say that the merest glimpse of him in the hall- way won't pierce your heart like a red-hot poker. But in time it won't hurt as much as it used to.

And then one day you will realize that it doesn't hurt *at all*, and that this other guy—the one you always liked but didn't think knew you were alive—actually liked you back all along, and the two of you will fall into each other's arms and live happily ever after. Even if you don't happen to be a princess.

TINA HAKIM BABA'S EXCLUSIVE INTERVIEW WITH AN ACTUAL GUY, ROYAL CONSORT MICHAEL MOSCOVITZ

Tina Hakim Baba: We are extremely fortunate to have been granted access to an actual live guy, Michael Moscovitz, who has agreed to a no-holds-barred interview on the topic of his love for Mia. Michael, first question: Would it be fair to say that your heart sang the first time you saw Mia?

Royal Consort
Michael Moscovitz: Um, well, technically, since the first time I laid eyes on Mia she was six years old, hanging upside down from a set of monkey bars, and her lips were blue because she'd just eaten a Rocket Pop, I would have to say, um, no.

Tina HBB: All right, well, when *did* you become aware that your life without Mia was an empty page, a blank book, a flimsy tissue of lies?

RC Michael M: Do I really have to answer this?

Tina HBB: You said no-holds-barred.

RC Michael M:	Well, then I would have to say the first time I saw her on in-line skates. Mia's the worst in-line skater I ever saw. She kept falling down. But then she'd get right back up again like nothing had happened. It was cute.
Tina HBB:	Cute?
RC Michael M:	Yeah. Cute.
Tina HBB:	Moving on. Does the breeze in the trees seem to sigh the word *Mia* as you walk by?
RC Michael M:	Not really.
Tina HBB:	It doesn't? Okay. But when your gaze meets Mia's, do you feel sparks inside?

RC Michael M:	You know what? I actually have to go. I have a thing. A thing to go to.
Tina HBB:	Just one more question: Which would you say attracted you to Mia most: a) Her mist-colored eyes b) Her tawny hair c) Her puckish yet highly kissable mouth or d) Her sylphlike figure
RC Michael M:	Um, I would have to say her sense of humor.
Tina HBB:	That is not one of the choices.
RC Michael M:	I know. But it's true.
Tina HBB:	I see. Well. Does every sinew in your being cry out to be reunited with your love when you are apart?
RC Michael M:	I really do have to go now.
Tina HBB:	Okay, but answer this first: Does Mia make you feel complete, fill a hole in yourself you didn't even know you had, make your lips tingle with a single look, inspire you to be better, more courageous, more giving, just to try to deserve her?
RC Michael M:	Um. Yes?
Tina HBB:	It has been a pleasure interviewing you, Michael. You are truly a man among men.

Conclusion

Princess Mia's Final Thoughts

A Note from
Her Royal Highness Princess Mia

I hope you have found this guide helpful. As you can see, there is a *lot* more to being a princess than just how to wear a tiara and pluck your eyebrows.

Just remember:

Kindness Counts Random acts of kindness rock! Instant messaging someone who seems down; offering to go to the movies with the new girl who no one likes; letting your best friend borrow your tiara to wear on her cable access television show—are all extremely princessy things to do.

Just Say No Thank You Just because you are kind does not mean you have to be a pushover. Don't let other people tell you what to do—unless what they are proposing is for your own good, like taking Algebra, or something. It is princesslike to be assertive. It is unprincesslike to be walked all over.

Smile Princesses always put their best face forward—not just because some reporter is probably going to jump out of the bushes and snap a picture of you and you don't want to be looking heinous when he does it, but for the good of your kingdom's morale. So you're a too-tall, flat-chested Japanese anime lover with a D-minus in Algebra, and the guy you adore isn't responding to the anonymous love letters you keep slipping into his locker. Never let your public see that any of it is bothering you! Don't be fake, but don't bring the kingdom down, either.

Always Be Gracious When we lose, we princesses don't let anyone know it bothers us. Instead, we go home and pour out all our hateful, jealous feelings into our diaries. So the guy you like appears to like a girl who knows how to clone fruit flies. So your best friend has a date to the Nondenominational Winter Dance and you don't. Don't let them know it bugs you! Princesses don't want anyone's pity.

And most important:

Be Yourself Princesses set their own trends, they don't follow the fashion dictates of others. Can a girl with green hair and a belly-button ring really be a princess? Absolutely, if she selected that green hair and belly-button ring because she wanted them, and not just because everyone else is wearing them.

Remember, being a princess is about how you act, not who your parents are, what kind of SAT scores you got, what extracurricular activities you choose to take part in, or how you look, in spite of what Grandmère, Sebastiano, Paolo, and everyone else says.

Being a princess is more of an attitude, really, than a way of life. And you know, even though there aren't enough countries on the planet for each one of us to get a chance to reign supreme, it's possible for all of us at least to *act* like a princess, even if some of you will never actually *be* one (and believe me, you are way better off that way).

Now go Rule!

YOU!

THE END

or possibly,
The Beginning?

M e g C a b o t is the author of the best-selling, critically acclaimed Princess Diaries books, the first of which was made into the wildly popular Disney movie of the same name. Her other books for teens include *All-American Girl*, *Haunted*, *Nicola and the Viscount*, and *Victoria and the Rogue*. When not writing novels, Meg keeps busy brushing up on her etiquette, so that when her real parents, the king and queen, come along and restore her to her rightful throne, she won't make any social gaffes. She lives in New York City with her royal consort and a one-eyed cat named Henrietta.

C h e s l e y M c L a r e n's work has graced the pages and windows of such fashionable clients as *Vogue*, *InStyle*, *The New York Times*, Saks Fifth Avenue, and Bergdorf Goodman. She debuted as an author/illustrator with *Zat Cat!, A Haute Couture Tail* and illustrated *You Forgot Your Skirt, Amelia Bloomer!* Though she could be quite happy living at Versailles among the chandeliers and ballrooms, Chesley resides in Manhattan with her royal consort and Monsieur Étoile, the original Zat Cat!